Winnie at Work

LAURA OWEN & KORKY PAUL

Helping your child to read

Before they start

★ Read the back cover blurb with your child. What do they think an after-school club run by Winnie would be like? Would it be fun?

★ What kind of food does your child think Winnie would cook for school dinner?

During reading

★ Let your child read at their own pace – don't worry if it's slow. Offer them plenty of help if they get stuck, and enjoy the story together.

★ Help them to work out words they don't know by saying each sound out loud and then blending them to say the word, e.g. *m-oa-n-i-n-g, moaning*.

★ If your child still struggles with a word, just tell them the word and move on.

★ Give them lots of praise for good reading!

After reading

★ Look at page 48 for some fun activities.

Contents

OXFORD
UNIVERSITY PRESS

Great Clarendon Street, Oxford OX2 6DP

Oxford University Press is a department of the University of Oxford.
It furthers the University's objective of excellence in research, scholarship,
and education by publishing worldwide. Oxford is a registered trade mark
of Oxford University Press in the UK and in certain other countries

"Shark in the Bath" was first published as "Winnie's After School Club" in *Winnie Spells Trouble*, 2014
"Disgusting Dinners" was first published as "Winnie's School Dinner" in *Winnie the Twit*, 2009

This edition published 2020

British Library Cataloguing in Publication Data

Data available

ISBN: 978-0-19-277375-3

1 3 5 7 9 10 8 6 4 2

Printed in China

Acknowledgements
With thanks to Caterine Baker for editorial support.

Shark in the Bath

Winnie had been busy all day.

She had done *lots* of boring jobs. She had cleaned the toilet . . . and the bath . . . and all her cauldrons.

"I want to do something interesting now!"
Winnie said. "What shall we do, Wilbur?"

But Wilbur was asleep.

Snore ...

Snore ...

SNORE!

"You're as boring as cleaning the toilet, Wilbur!" said Winnie.

Just then, Winnie's moaning phone rang.

Moany-moan-squeak-eek!

It was Mrs Parmar at the school. She was in a terrible tizzy!

"Help me, Winnie!" cried Mrs Parmar. "I need you to run the after-school club! Come quickly, or there will be no one to look after the children!"

"How witchy wonderful!" said Winnie. "We love playing with the children, don't we, Wilbur?"

So they jumped on the broomstick.

whizzzzzz!

The after-school club children were playing happily.

"I'll only be gone for one hour," said Mrs Parmar.
"But you are NOT to do any magic on the
children, Winnie."

"Of course not!" smiled Winnie.

As soon as Mrs Parmar had gone, Winnie started playing.

Winnie climbed up the climbing frame and hung upside d$_{o_{w_{n_!}}}$

Then, she jumped on the seesaw.

Wheeee!

Clonk!   Bump!

She sent a boy called Max flying!

Max landed on top of a girl called Daisy.

Daisy fell over, and knocked into Charlie.

Then everyone fell over! Some of the children started crying.

Waaah!

"I know what we need!" said Winnie.

"Snack-a-roos!"

Winnie got her bag. She took out cockroach crispies, slimy wormy sandwiches and a jug of cactus crush.

"Yuck!" shouted the children. Then they all started crying!

Waaah! Waaah! Waaah!

But then Winnie had a good idea. "Don't worry, Wilbur," she said. "I won't use magic on the children. I'll use it on something else."

She waved her wand. "**Abracadabra!**"

At once, all the toys in the playground came to life.

The football was bouncing on its own!

B-o-u-n-c-e!

Suddenly, there were real monkeys playing on the climbing frame.

The toy cars turned into real cars. The toy ponies started trotting round the playground.

For a moment, all the children were silent.

Then Max said, "That's magic!"

Everybody started cheering. They rushed around and played with all the toys and animals.

The noise was amazing!

Just then, Winnie saw Mrs Parmar coming back.
Quickly, Winnie waved her wand under her
cardigan. "Abracadabra!" she whispered.

Mrs Parmar looked at Winnie. "I hope everything went well," she said.

"YES!" shouted the children. "Can Winnie look after us tomorrow?"

"I've had enough noise for one week!" said Winnie.

Winnie and Wilbur whizzed home as fast as they could.

"At last we can relax, Wilbur!" Winnie grabbed the frogspawn bubble bath. "This is just what I need," she said. "A nice, relaxing bath!"

"It was fun when the toys came alive," thought

Winnie in her bath. So she waved her wand.

"**Abracadabra!**"

All Winnie's bath toys came alive.

"Ouch!" shouted Winnie. "That's my toe!"

She had forgotten all about her toy shark!

Winnie jumped out of the bath.

"Never mind, Wilbur," she said. "We'll have some lovely hot chocolate. The frogspawn bubbles from the bath will make a great topping!"

"Meeow!" said Wilbur, happily.

Disgusting Dinners

"I spy, with my little eye, something beginning with 'w'," said Winnie.

Wilbur pointed at her.

"No, not Winnie!" said Winnie. "Not witch, either. Try again!"

Wilbur sighed. He pointed at Winnie's wand.

"Yes!" said Winnie. "It's 'w' for wand! Come on, Wilbur. I spy, with my little eye, something else beginning with 'w'."

Wilbur gave a big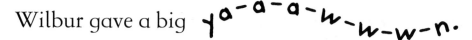

"Wobbling walruses, you're right, Wilbur!" said Winnie. "This is boring! I only know 'w'. I'd better go to school and learn some more letters!"

So Winnie and Wilbur went to school.

There were lots of children playing in the playground.

"This will be fun, Wilbur!" said Winnie.

But Mrs Parmar didn't need Winnie's help.

"We've already got helpers in the school today," she said. "Off you go!"

Winnie and Wilbur turned round to go home.
Just then, they saw someone waving to them. It was
the school cook.

"There are lots of mice in the kitchen," she said.
"Can you catch them for me, Wilbur?"

So Wilbur jumped through the kitchen window.

Eeek! Squeak! Tweak!

He caught three mice in one go.

"Well done!" said the cook. "You can work here and catch mice every day!"

"Oh!" said Winnie. "Can I work here, too?"

"Are you good at cooking?" asked the cook.

"Slippery slugs!" said Winnie. "Of course I am! Just wait till you taste my slimy sn—"

But Wilbur put his paw over her mouth just in time.

"Good," said the cook. "You can work here, too, then."

She gave Winnie a proper cook's apron and hat.

"I've got to go now," she said. "You can make the school lunch, Winnie. It's stew and pasta. Good luck!"

Wilbur looked in all the cupboards. But he couldn't find any meat for the stew.

"Oh well," said Winnie. "Catch some mice and rats, Wilbur. We can use those."

So Wilbur raced off to catch some meat for the stew.

"We need to cook some pasta, too," said Winnie.

"What shall I use for the sauce?"

Winnie thought for a bit. "I know – worms!"
she said. "They make a lovely sauce with some
cucumber!"

So she went out to the playground.

"**Abracadabra!**"

At once she had a big bucket of wriggly worms.

Soon Winnie and Wilbur were back in the kitchen, cooking as fast as they could.

Mix! Stir! Pour!

Clang-clang! It was the dinner bell.

In the dining hall, everyone was lining up for dinner.

Mrs Parmar was surprised to see Winnie, but she was hungry. "I'll have a big bowl of pasta, please," she said.

"Eat up!" said Winnie. "It's worm and cucumber pasta!"

"Yuck! That's disgusting!" Mrs Parmar spat out her first mouthful and ran out of the hall.

None of the children wanted Winnie's pasta or the rat stew either.

"What would you like to eat, then?" asked Winnie.

"Doughnuts!" said one boy.

"Cake!" said a girl. **Yum!**

So Winnie got out her wand. "**Abracadabra!**"

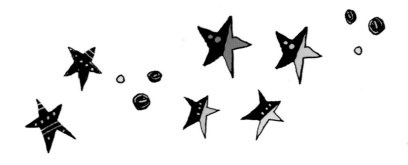

The rat stew changed into doughnuts.

The worm pasta turned into delicious cakes.

"Hooray!" shouted the children.

"Hooray!"

"Hooray!"

But then Mrs Parmar came back in. She was *not* pleased.

"Winnie, will you please clear up this unhealthy food?"

Afterwards, Winnie and Wilbur went home.

"Oh well, Wilbur," said Winnie. "I've learned one useful thing at school today."

"Meeow?" asked Wilbur.

"A new letter! I spy with my little eye, something beginning with 'q'!"

"Meeow?" asked Wilbur again.

"Look, it's a cucumber!" said Winnie.

"Meeeowwww!" groaned Wilbur, tucking into his dinner. At least Winnie's cooking was better than her spelling!

After reading activities

Talk about the stories

Ask your child the following questions. Encourage them to talk about their answers.

1) In "Shark in the Bath", what goes wrong when Winnie does some magic in the bath?

2) In "Disgusting Dinners", why does Winnie decide to go to school?

3) In "Disgusting Dinners", do you think Mrs Parmar is right to be cross with Winnie?

1) The toy shark bites her; 2) To learn some more letters; 3) Open question – child's own opinion.

Try this!

If one of your toys came alive, what might happen? What would you do together? Act out the scene or draw a picture.